Oliver's Tree

Kit Chase

G. P. PUTNAM'S SONS
An Imprint of Penguin Group (USA)

To Mummy and Pop,
my best chum Adam,
and my sweetest little friends:
Pearly, Gwynnie, and Lucy
(and those I've still yet to meet!)

Lulu

Oliver

Charlie

Once, there were three friends.

They loved to play outside.

"Ready or not, here I come!" said Oliver.

Oliver spotted Lulu. He jumped and jumped.
But he couldn't reach her.

"That's not fair," said Oliver.
"Trees are out of bounds."

"But trees are the best
hiding spots!" cried Lulu.

"Not all trees are the same,"
Charlie said. "We'll find
a tree you can play in, too."

So they found another tree.
"Look," said Lulu. "This one's low
to the ground so you can climb it."

But it was too small. Oliver couldn't fit.

So they found *another* tree.
"Try this one," said Charlie.
"The branches are bigger."

But it was too tall.
Oliver still couldn't reach his friends.

So they found one more tree.

"Perfect!" Lulu said. "We can help you up."

And it was just right.

Until . . .

"It's hopeless!" cried Oliver.

"Elephants just don't belong in trees!"

Oliver walked until he was too tired
to take another step.

When Lulu and Charlie found him,
Oliver was fast asleep.

"Poor Oliver," said Charlie.

"He's so sad. I wish we could help him."

"I have a plan," said Lulu.

Lulu searched high

and Charlie searched low.
They gathered sticks and moss
and pawfuls of leaves.

Then they rolled and patted

and tinkered and nudged, until everything was perfect.

"Surprise!" they shouted
when Oliver woke up.
"Where am I?" asked Oliver.
"In a tree!" said Charlie.

"It's not too small and not too tall," Lulu said.
"It's a tree house. Perfect for all of us!"
"Hurray!" trumpeted Oliver.

"This is the best tree in the world!"

G. P. PUTNAM'S SONS
Published by The Penguin Group
Penguin Group (USA) LLC
375 Hudson Street
New York, NY 10014

USA | Canada | UK | Ireland | Australia | New Zealand | India | South Africa | China
penguin.com
A Penguin Random House Company

Library of Congress Cataloging-in-Publication Data
Chase, Kit. Oliver's tree / Kit Chase.
pages cm
Summary: Oliver the elephant loves playing hide-and-seek but cannot tag his friends, Lulu and Charlie, when they
hide in trees—their favorite spots—so they work together to find a tree where all three can play together.
[1. Hide-and-seek—Fiction. 2. Friendship—Fiction. 3. Elephants—Fiction. 4. Owls—Fiction. 5. Rabbits—Fiction.] I. Title.
PZ7.C38732Oli
2014 [E]—dc23
2013014667
Manufactured in China by South China Printing Co. Ltd.
ISBN 978-0-399-25700-1
3 5 7 9 10 8 6 4 2

Design by Annie Ericsson. Text set in Cooper Oldstyle Light.
The art was done in watercolor with pen and ink.